For Kait, who saw something
sweet in Panda. —B.S.

Clarion Books is an imprint of HarperCollins Publishers.

Cindy and Panda
Copyright © 2023 by Benson Shum
All rights reserved. Manufactured in Italy.
No part of this book may be used or reproduced in any manner
whatsoever without written permission except in the case of
brief quotations embodied in critical articles and reviews.
For information address HarperCollins Children's Books, a division
of HarperCollins Publishers, 195 Broadway, New York, NY 10007.
www.harpercollinschildrens.com

ISBN 978-0-06-324818-2

The artist used watercolor and ink and compiled them in Photoshop
to create the digital illustrations for this book.
Typography by Whitney Leader-Picone
Recipe by Allison Chi, tested by Lois Evans,
David Newton, and Penny Leader-Picone
23 24 25 26 27 RTLO 10 9 8 7 6 5 4 3 2 1

First Edition

CINDY and Panda

SWEET PIES

Benson Shum

Clarion Books | *An Imprint of HarperCollinsPublishers*

Cindy loved to bake!
But she didn't always follow a recipe.
She liked to do things her own way.

Today she was making her favorite—sweet rhubarb pie!

She flew off to the garden to pick the filling . . .

...and came back with something sweeter.

"Cindy," said her mother. "We're not having panda pie."
"We're not eating my friend!" said Cindy. "Panda wants to help bake!"
"Pandas are a huge responsibility," warned Mother.

"I'm responsible!" Cindy replied with her sweetest smile.

Responsible Cindy showed
her new sous-chef around.

Playing is a very important
part of pie preparation.
After hours of rolling around ...

. . . a tummy rumbled.
"Uh-oh! We should get
started!" said Cindy.

Cindy made sure to show
Panda the proper steps:

Step 1. Measure the sugar.

Step 2. Pour the flour.

Step 3...

Fre
St

Cindy and Panda were proud of their work.

They just needed to add the final ingredient!

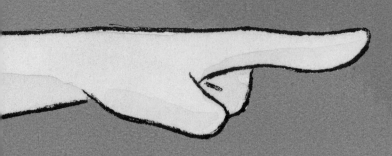

Cindy soured.
Panda soured too.

Cindy couldn't
bear to look at
Panda for hours.

Well, more like
three minutes.

But it was the longest
and loneliest three
minutes ever.

Then Cindy had a berry good idea.

Blueberries!

They're sweet.

And tart.

And, at times, a little bit sour.
Just like Cindy and Panda.

But everybody loves them, just the same.

Cindy and Panda's Blueberry Pie
by Allison Chi

Ingredients

Crust
- 2½ cups flour
- ½ teaspoon cinnamon
- ⅛ teaspoon salt
- 2 sticks butter, cold
- ice water
- 1 egg
- 1 tablespoon water

Filling
- 3 pints blueberries
- Juice and zest of 1 lemon
- ½ teaspoon vanilla extract
- ¾ cup white sugar
- 3 tablespoons cornstarch
- 1 teaspoon cinnamon
- ¼ teaspoon fine sea salt

Make the Crust

Mix the flour, cinnamon, and salt in a large bowl. Cut the butter into cubes and smoosh flat, about the size of a blueberry, then add to the bowl. Add 8 tbsp of ice water. Toss until the water is absorbed and the mixture forms a ball. If needed, add 1 tbsp more at a time. Divide the ball into two pieces and shape each into a disc about 3" wide and 1" tall. Wrap them in plastic wrap and refrigerate them for at least one hour.

Make the Pie

Preheat the oven to 425°. Roll out the chilled dough into two 10" discs. Place the first disc into a pie dish and press the sides. There should be about 1" of overhang. Mix the blueberries, lemon juice and zest, and vanilla extract in a small bowl. In a medium bowl, whisk together the sugar, cornstarch, cinnamon, and salt. Now combine the bowls! Pour the filling into the pie dish, then lay the second dough disc on top. Crimp the edges by pinching the outside of the pie. With a knife, score a 3" X in the middle. Beat the egg with the water and brush it on top of the crust (but not the edges!). Bake for 20 minutes. Lower the temperature to 350° and bake for 55–70 more minutes. The pie is ready when the filling is bubbling and the crust is golden brown. Let the pie cool for at least an hour. Eat with ice cream, or freestyle in your own way!